Class Trip

Class Trip

Robert Munsch

illustrations by
Michael Martchenko

North Winds Press
An Imprint of Scholastic Canada Ltd.

The art for this book was painted in watercolour on Crescent illustration board.
The type is set in 18 point Minister Std.

www.scholastic.ca

Library and Archives Canada Cataloguing in Publication

Title: Class trip / Robert Munsch ; illustrations by Michael Martchenko.
Names: Munsch, Robert N., 1945- author. | Martchenko, Michael, illustrator.
Description: Published simultaneously in softcover by Scholastic Canada Ltd.
Identifiers: Canadiana 20230223214 | ISBN 9781039702233 (hardcover)
Classification: LCC PS8576.U575 C55 2023 | DDC jC813/.54—dc23

8 7 6 5 4 3 2 1   Printed in Canada 114   23 24 25 26 27 28 29

For Stephanie Gangl,
Toronto, Ontario.
— R.M.

One day, Stephanie and Sean went
with all the other kids to a museum.

The man at the museum said, "Hey, you can watch chickens come out of eggs!"

"Wonderful," said Stephanie.

So Stephanie and Sean sat and looked at the eggs and looked at the eggs and looked at the eggs and all of a sudden one of them cracked open and out came a baby chicken.

5

"Neat!" said Sean. "Got any bigger eggs?"

"Why, yes," said the man, "look over here. We've got turkey eggs."

They were really big.

So Stephanie and Sean sat and sat and sat and sat and sat and sat and sat and sat and finally the egg cracked open and out came a baby turkey.

"Wonderful!" said Stephanie. "Got anything bigger?"

"Yes," said the man, "we have ostrich eggs. Ostrich eggs! Look at this! Really big eggs!"

So they sat and sat and sat and sat and sat and sat and sat and sat and just when they got really bored the egg cracked and out came a baby ostrich.

"Well," said Sean, "what's the biggest egg you've got?"

"Oh my," said the man. "Well, down in the basement, and I don't usually show this, is a very big egg. We are not even sure what it is from."

So Stephanie and Sean went down to the basement. There was an ENORMOUS egg, but it was already cracked open.

"Wow!" said Stephanie. "It looks like a dinosaur egg."

They looked and looked and looked but they could not find a giant chick, so they went to look at the eggshell.

"Amazing!" said Sean.

"I bet," said Stephanie, "that I could fit inside that egg."

"No," said Sean.

"Yes," said Stephanie.

"No," said Sean.

"Yes!" said Stephanie. "Watch."

She jumped in half the egg and put the other half over her head.

Sean said, "It's amazing! Stay there. I'll glue it back together."

So he glued the egg back together and just then the teacher came in and said, "Where's Stephanie?"

"I don't know," said Sean, "but I'm listening to this egg. It can talk."

"Eggs can't talk," said the teacher.

"Put your ear to the egg," said Sean.

The teacher put her ear to the egg and Stephanie said, "Hello."

"Oh no!" said the teacher. "It talked! This is amazing. An egg talks!"

"And," said Sean, "it can add. Egg, what is 2 plus 2?"

The egg said, "It's 4."

"Incredible!" said the teacher. "This egg is smarter than the kids in my class. This is amazing. I'm going to see how smart it really is."

She looked at the egg and said, "Egg, how much is 5 times 5?"

The egg said, "That's 25."

"Wow!" said the teacher. "Egg, how much is 252 divided by 18?"

"Duhhhhh . . ." said the egg.

"Aaawww," said the teacher, "you're not that smart at all."

Stephanie jumped out of the egg and said, "I am very smart!"

The teacher was so surprised she fainted.

"You know," said Stephanie, "maybe we could fit the teacher in the egg."

"Good idea," said Sean.

They took the two pieces of egg, put them around the teacher and glued it all together. When the teacher's aide came down to find them they said, "Look, they said we could have this big egg."

So they took the egg back to school and put it inside the classroom, and the teacher's aide went to find the principal.

The principal came and said, "All right, where's your teacher? She didn't come back from the museum."

"We don't know where the teacher is, but look at this egg," said Sean. "It can talk."

"Eggs can't talk," said the principal. He went over to the egg, knocked on it and said, "Hello."

A voice from inside the egg said, "Hello?"

"Oh no," said the principal. "It's an egg and it can talk."

"It's more than that," said Sean. "It can do math."

"Yo, egg, how much is 2 plus 2?" said the principal.

"It's 4," said the egg.

"It can add. It's smarter than the teachers at this school. I'm gonna see how smart it really is, though," said the principal. "Egg, how much is 9 times 12?"

"That's 108," said the egg.

"Okay, then," said the principal. "How much is 436 divided by 109 times 15 plus 32 minus 1?"

"Ummmm . . . 3?" said the egg.

"Ha! You are not a smart egg at all," said the principal.

The teacher jumped out of the egg and said, "I am a very smart egg!"

The principal ran screaming back to his office and the teacher spent the whole rest of the day trying to figure out 436 divided by 109 times 15 plus 32 minus 1.